Merry Christmas
to
Aunt Ethel & Uncle Lyle

love,

Larry, Carol
Brady & Taghe
1986

THE MYSTERIOUS TOYSHOP

THE MYSTERIOUS TOYSHOP

A Fairy Tale

by

CYRIL W. BEAUMONT

With Decorations

by

WYNDHAM PAYNE

THE METROPOLITAN MUSEUM OF ART
HOLT, RINEHART AND WINSTON
NEW YORK

THIS BOOK is a facsimile of the first edition of *The Mysterious Toyshop* published in London by Cyril W. Beaumont in 1924. A copy of the first edition is in the collection of the Department of Prints and Photographs of The Metropolitan Museum of Art.

Published in 1985 by
The Metropolitan Museum of Art and
Holt, Rinehart and Winston
All rights reserved
Produced by The Department of Special Publications,
The Metropolitan Museum of Art
Printed and bound by A. Mondadori, Verona, Italy
ISBN 0-87099-429-8 The Metropolitan Museum of Art
ISBN 0-03-005852-X Holt, Rinehart and Winston

Library of Congress Cataloging in Publication Data
Beaumont, Cyril W. (Cyril William), 1891-1976.
    The mysterious toyshop.
    Summary: A new toyshop, full of wonderful dolls and miniatures for both children and adults, is found to harbor an amazing secret.
    [1. Toys—Fiction. 2. Dolls—Fiction. 3. Stores, Retail—Fiction] I. Payne, Wyndham, ill. II. Title.
PZ7.B38079My   1985   [Fic]   85-11555
ISBN 0-87099-429-8

For ALICE SCHWABE

THE MYSTERIOUS TOYSHOP

IT was a fortnight before Christmas, and every one agreed that this would be a real Christmas, such as had not been seen for many years. There was a delightful cold nip in the air, as exhilarating as good news ; the sky was grey and overcast, and the streets were covered with a thick layer of snow.

Few sights are more charming than that of a town covered with new-fallen, clean, white snow ; and how pretty it is to watch the tiny flakes drift downward through the air as if there were a wedding in the sky and the fairies were throwing confetti.

At this time of the year the afternoons are short and the daylight quickly fades, so that the narrow streets which lead off the main roads of a great city like London assume an air more and more mysterious. The passer-by looks anxiously about him .as his business takes him down some dark alley, for this is the season of goblins and pixies and elves—perhaps even the will-o'-the-wisps are in town.

This is not a story of to-day but of fifty years ago, when ladies wore bustles and full skirts reaching to the ground ; when gentlemen favoured whiskers, and horses had no difficulty in finding steady employment ; while at night the streets were dimly lighted with flames of gas, quivering in tall lamp-posts set far apart. Every Londoner knows the quaint streets which run each side of the thoroughfare of Holborn, and in one of these was situated the toyshop that is the subject of our tale.   It would not be well to mention the street by name, for you might be tempted to search for the shop, which, alas, exists no longer.

It sprang into being almost as quickly as the magic palace of Aladdin.   Nothing was known of its past history, and, truth to tell, very little of its arrival.   A neighbour remembered when the shop, with its two upper floors, was empty.   He had even thought of taking it himself, but, while he was still meditating as to whether he could extend his business with profit, there appeared in the window a square strip of paper on which was printed in bold characters the single word LET.

In a few days the shop was open.   More than one neighbour commented on the extraordinary quickness and secrecy with which the alterations had been carried out.   There was none of the usual screeching of saws and tapping of hammers associated with the opening of a new business. No workmen had been seen, nor had carts drawn up to unload great wooden cases marked THIS SIDE UP.

Yet the shop was open ; and how splendid it

looked ! The whitening had been cleaned from the large window so that, for the first time for weeks, one could look through its panes. And what treasures were to be seen ! There were games of chess and draughts ; cricket bats and shuttlecocks ; little chipwood boxes labelled Sparkling Snow, boxes of Bengal lights ; all kinds of gaily-painted lead foot-soldiers with horsemen and cannons to match ; Noah's Arks filled with the strangest animals ; toy guns, pistols and swords ; infantry shakoes, Lancer czapkas, Hussar busbies and even Life Guardsman helmets, with real horse-hair plumes, for young soldiers ; wooden horses, forts, and turreted castles with a moat that could be filled with water and a fine drawbridge which could be let down for the garrison to pass across without getting wet ; spinning tops and humming tops ; stuffed leather balls of all sizes and colours ; boats with sails to carry them over pond and lake ; dolls of china, wood and wax, with houses for them to live in, all complete with furniture for the bedroom and drawing-room, while there was even a kitchen fitted with plates and dishes, cooking utensils and a tiny brush and dust-pan.

There were books of Fairy Tales, model theatres with scenery and real footlights ; packs of cards and boxes of conjuring tricks ; magic mirrors which, when breathed upon, displayed a bright flower on their surface ; and magic eggs which, when lighted, would hatch a writhing brown serpent. But all these were only a few of the wonders to be seen. Few passers-by could avoid the absorbing attraction of the

windows ; and, jutting over the doorway, was a jolly sign in the form of a miniature Christmas tree, its branches hung with little tinkling bells that enticed people walking in the streets near-by.

Grown-up men and women would laugh and smile on seeing the gay windows ; for the toys awakened memories of childhood long forgotten amid years of toil, so that they felt quite young again, and thought once more of the joy of spinning tops, of playing with toy theatres and lead soldiers, and of the rapture of making dolly's clothes and dressing her to be taken in her perambulator for an airing in the park.

Children would clap their hands with delight and their little hearts ached with longing to possess the treasures so temptingly displayed. Carefully-brought-up young ladies, with rosy cheeks and dainty curls, dressed in fine fur coats and caps to keep them warm, became naughty and discontented and stamped their feet if their mammas did not stop to take them inside.

There passed other little girls, sometimes holding the hand of a smaller brother or sister,

just as pretty, but with un-tidy hair, pale faces and wearing torn cotton frocks. For a long while they would remain looking in at the window, their noses pressed against the cold glass. They would point eagerly to one

object after another. One
adored this doll because of
her bright blue eyes, another
favoured that one for her long
golden curls ; the little boy hun-
gered for a box of soldiers.
Then they would become sad,
for they knew that they could

not afford anything, not even a penny box of
Serpent's Eggs. The little group would move
slowly homewards to talk in whispers of what
they had seen, and of what they would do, if
only Uncle Tom sent them at Christmas a
whole half-a-crown as he had done last year.
Within a few days of its opening, the shop was
well started on a prosperous career. Indulgent
parents had been over to visit the much talked-
of shop, and even the poor children, by running
errands, holding horses' heads and selling empty
bottles and jam-jars, had scraped together pre-
cious coppers which they brought to spend,
carefully wrapped up in a knotted handker-
chief.

Now and again broughams and hansoms
would drive up with a great clatter of hooves
and rattle of wheels. One could always tell the
new customers, for they
would loiter about the
windows and hesitate, as if
undecided to enter. Then
they would make up their
minds and go in, to re-
appear, seldom less than an
hour later, carrying many
neat parcels tied up with

pink tape. But those who had already paid a visit to the shop would enter briskly, with a pleasant smile on their faces, as if calling on an old friend.

The inside of the shop was more wonderful even than the window. It was a long rambling room, full of bends and corners that seemed to say : " You'll lose yourself if you're not careful." The first object to meet the eye was a large doll placed just inside the doorway. It was dressed as a fairy in a beautiful costume of white muslin and silver. Its hair was tied with a white silk ribbon which served to support a silver star, one arm was outstretched and held a silver wand which pointed towards a long glass-covered counter, heaped with objects to tempt the most exacting child. The walls were lined with shelves and cases full of toys and brightly coloured boxes, with their lids raised ever so slightly to afford a tantalising peep at the treasures within. The ceiling was dazzling in its light and colour, for it was covered with convex and concave mirrors, so that to look upward was to see oneself distorted into a thousand queer shapes. Where the mirrors joined there were suspended rows of paper lanterns each containing a lighted candle, silver globes, toy balloons and droll animals strung on elastic thread, so that they were continually twisting and turning and dancing up and down.

At a little distance from the counter was a big tub in which stood a Christmas tree. Its branches were hung with little nets, in the form of stockings, filled with sweets, puzzles and tricks ; trumpets and tiny drums ; bonbons and white sugar mice with bright pink ears and noses ; and small dolls and whistles ; while quite a hundred red, blue, green and orange candles were fastened to the branches, each burning as brightly as could be.

The customers were served by two assistants as quaint as the toys themselves. They were both young men, dressed quietly in dark clothes. Both wore high and very clean collars, tied with bright blue cravats ; their crisp hair was neatly parted in the middle and their faces were as bright and rosy as if they had been freshly scraped. Their eyes did not appear to move, for they invariably stared in front of them or jerked their heads to right or left ; their hands were pale and well kept, and their movements angular and spasmodic, as if they had absorbed something of the nature of the toys which surrounded them. They did not appear to have any names, being always known as No. 1 and No. 2.

They were very restricted in their conversation, which was limited to the quotation of the price of a particular toy and phrases like : " Very seasonable, sir," " Very charming, sir," " Very realistic, sir," and " No, sir," or " Yes, sir ; " the " sir " being changed to " madam " as occasion demanded. The customers were grateful for this brevity ; they did not wish to have anything pressed upon them. They much preferred to roam about the shop and make their selection at leisure.

A flight of stairs at the end of the shop led to the upper rooms, of which, as we have said already, there were two. That on the first floor

was used as a stock-room and filled with cardboard boxes. At the end of this room was another staircase which led to the top floor of all. This was occupied by the proprietor himself, an old man, clad in check trousers and coat and waistcoat of black velvet. His head was covered with brown hair, slightly tinged with silver, which stuck up in the most amazing way. He walked in a precise and deliberate manner, while his hands, pale almost to transparency, performed curious gesticulations.

The walls of the room were covered with a striped paper, the floor was spread with a brightly patterned carpet. One wall was lined with shelves on which was disposed an extraordinary collection of the various parts of a doll's anatomy. There were heads of every shape and size in china, wood and wax ; strands of hair of all shades ; arms, legs and bodies, some stuffed, some of carved wood, some of china, some cast in wax and various compositions. There were boxes of springs and screws, wheels toothed and plain, and all manner of nuts and bolts.

Against the opposite wall stood a large glass case holding a collection of magnificent dolls and toys. The remaining wall was hung with designs for dolls and against the window, which was of frosted

glass, stood a broad bench fitted with a rack holding tools. Over the window hung two cages fashioned of brass wire, each containing a pretty green bird which, by some hidden mechanism, continually hopped on its perch, preened its wings and sang so sweetly that one seemed to hear the music of a plashing fountain or the tinkle of tiny glass bells. The centre of the room was occupied by a comfortable leather chair and a large table littered with plans and pieces of mechanism.

Very rarely did the proprietor leave the room. All day long and at night too, when the neighbours were fast asleep, he laboured at the perfection of his dolls and toys. He seldom descended into the shop to converse with a customer. But, now and again, when a respected client had called to express his thanks for the delight which his purchases had procured his children, or had been especially complimentary, one of the assistants would glide to his side and, whispering nervously into his ear, inquire if he would like to see some particularly fine dolls —suitable for grown-ups. At the suggestion of new marvels, the customer scarcely dared to breathe for fear of losing a word and, nodding his head, would inquire, in the calmest voice he could assume, where they could be seen. Thereupon, the assistant would beckon to him, and together they would climb the winding staircase past the stock-room and up to the top floor, where the proprietor lived.

Hearing an unfamiliar footstep, the old man would look up angrily from his work, but, seeing before him only the half-enraptured,

half-mystified countenance of the customer, he would greet him with a smile, and with a wave of his hand, introduce him to what he was pleased to call his children. But when the customer heard the melodious voices of the birds, and his eyes rested on the contents of the glass case, he could hardly speak, so great was his astonishment and joy.

The old man would tilt his head on one side, slowly finger his chin, and, steadfastly regarding his visitor, seek to fathom his tastes. The stock was choice, the selection wide. Then he would open the case and his hands would stray lovingly over the shelves to come to rest on some object which he would take out with great care, and set down on the table, unless it were one of the larger dolls, when it would be stood upon the floor. There were little ducks that swam round on a pool of glass, a miniature blacksmith who beat his hammer on an anvil with engaging rhythm. Now a coach containing a fine lady who flirted at the window behind her raised fan ; the coach was drawn by six high-stepping horses driven by a coachman who, at intervals, cracked his whip. Then there were two knights who ran a course, each horse in turn being forced on its haunches as its rider was thrown back under the impact of the victor's lance.

Perhaps he would take one of the large dolls, an acrobat maybe, a handsome youth in tights and tunic covered with glittering spangles, who would leap, stand on his head and perform

somersaults with incredible facility ; then a
player of the pipe and tabor, dressed in silk and
satin just as if he had stepped from one of
Lancret's paintings. Between his lips was a
little pipe, and when a small lever in his hat was
turned, he played upon the pipe with the fingers
of his left hand, while his right held a stick with
which he beat his drum. Sometimes, it would
be a doll dressed as a famous dancer, her
features, her limbs, her skirt all so exact, that
for the moment the customer blushed to find
himself face to face with Taglioni. Concealed
in her body was a musical box which played the
sad air from *La Sylphide*. Then the dancer's
arms would rise in a delightful curve, and she
would glide to and fro on her toes in so graceful
a manner that the onlooker thought himself
seated in a theatre. When the music ceased,
the dancer would make a sweeping curtsey as
if in response to the clamours of an appreciative
audience, and the proprietor would come for-
ward, pat her tightly dressed hair, and return
her to the case.

The customer would itch to possess all these
marvels, but the old man touched his creations
so reverently that he would be at a loss how to
broach so vulgar a subject as that of price. To
gain time, he would utter a profusion of thanks,
and then, conscious that he had outstayed his
welcome, throw caution to the winds and,
instead of the nicely turned phrase he had
planned, blurt out :—

" Are they for sale ? "

" Yes and no," would be the answer. " If
you wish for the coach or the acrobat, yes ; but

Taglioni, no, I cannot part with her to-day.
Perhaps to-morrow, or the day after."

The more pressing the customer became, the
more evasive would be the old man's replies.
Then the customer, fearful of being unable to
buy anything, would purchase the coach or the
acrobat.   The proprietor would smile sadly,
wrap up the object and, bowing the customer
out, see him safely to the ground floor and bid
him good-day with a shake of the hand.

" What a strange shop," mused the customer
on his way home.   " What a peculiar man.
And how cold his hands were."

And every night when he had returned to his
house and put on his slippers, dined well and
toasted his feet before the fire, he would show
his purchase to an admiring circle composed of
his family and such friends as had dropped in.

The wonder of the toys was talked of every-
where.   It became the fashion to send out
invitation cards for lunch or dinner with one
corner bearing the inscription :—

To see a purchase from the new toyshop.

The customary R.S.V.P. was omitted, for

who could refuse so singu-
lar an attraction ? " Have
you seen the new toy-
shop ? " was the first
question at every social
function. Ladies chat-
tered volubly about it at
their " tea-parties." Even
grave city gentlemen were

known to interrupt important business meetings
with the familiar phrase : " Have you seen the
new toyshop ? " It was always spoken of as " the
new toyshop," because neither the window nor
the façia bore a name, only the legend DOLLS
& TOYS.

The shop was not easy to find, and it was
never known to advertise ; yet its ground floor
was always thronged with customers. Few of
these attained to their ambition of being able
to boast that they had visited the wonderful
top floor. Those who, on entering, stamped
impatiently on the floor ; those who, after
waiting barely two minutes, shouted : " Is
there no one to attend to me ? " ; those who,
in their clumsiness, upset the neat piles of
boxes on the counter and never troubled to
replace a single one ; those who, on being
acquainted with the price of a toy, cried :
" Stuff and nonsense, I can obtain this any-
where at a quarter of what you ask,"—not one
of these, I fear, even so much as set foot on the
stair that led to the top floor.

And then came the incident which brought
grief to so many lovers of toys. A gentleman
of considerable importance, whose name shall

not be mentioned, was shown a dancer doll at the house of an acquaintance.

" Bless my soul ! " he gasped, " where did you get that ? "

" At the new toyshop," was the answer.

" Most amusing, I must certainly get one too."

" It's not so easy," said his host, " unless you're a well-known customer there—and even that is no guarantee that one of the assistants will present you to the proprietor."

" But surely," remonstrated the other, " it is possible to buy such a doll in the shop without the extraordinary formality of being presented to the proprietor ? "

" On the contrary, dolls of this kind can be purchased only from the proprietor, who works in a strange room on the top floor."

" And of what use, pray, is a shop where the goods are not for sale ? "

" I admit it's unusual, but then this is an unusual kind of shop."

" Come, come, my dear sir, I have never yet met with a shop where the stock is for show and not for sale. It's pure humbug—another one of these new-fangled ideas for advertisement." During this speech, he took out his snuff-box and underlined his words with sundry taps of his finger-nail upon the lid, after which he opened the box, took a pinch of the contents and proffered the box to his companion.

The next day he ordered his carriage and instructed his coachman to drive him to the shop. Presently the carriage drew up in a narrow street. The gentleman alighted, entered the shop, and boldly making his way to the counter, stopped in front of No. 1. He presented his card, which bore a well-known name, and inquired :

" Can I see the proprietor ? "

" Engaged, sir," was the response.

" Will he be at liberty shortly ? "

" Cannot say, sir," replied No. 1.

" Very well, I will call another day."

He stamped out, stepped into his carriage, and was driven home in a disgruntled state at his rebuff, for there were few places to which the production of his card did not secure his immediate admittance.

He called the next day with the same result. He missed a day, and ventured again ; only to receive the same reply. Then, just as he was about to voice his displeasure, he saw an evident customer descending the stairs escorted by a dignified old man. " This," he thought, " must be the proprietor." He quietly made his way to that end of the shop and pretended to be interested in the contents of a case, while the customer, with many expressions of thanks, took his departure. Then the stranger approached the old man and asked :

" Are you the proprietor ? "

" That is so," was the reply.

He was astonished at the dignity of his bearing and the formal politeness of his tone, so different from the servility to which he was accustomed. Then, in the suavest voice, he inquired :

" May I have the pleasure of a few minutes' conversation with you ? "

" I am very busy," said the old man, " and

I rarely see strangers. However, in this case,"
he added graciously, " I shall be happy to make
an exception. Will you please come upstairs ? "

"Confound his impudence," thought the
Stranger, but eagerly followed him.

Arrived at the top floor, the proprietor turned
to his visitor and remarked :

"Pardon this disorder, but, as you see, this
is my work-room. And now, what is your
pleasure ? "

A few seconds passed before the Stranger
spoke, he was so astonished at the sight of the
wonderful toys. He was all eagerness to possess
them.

"I wish to purchase some of your better
toys," he answered. " I will make a selection
and if you will inform me of the prices, I will
write you out a cheque—on the Bank of Eng-
land—for the amount."

"I greatly appreciate your kindness," said
the old man, " but here I have nothing for
sale."

The Stranger began to frown.

"Am I to understand," he inquired, with a

shade of sarcasm in his tone, " that in this shop the goods are not for sale ? "

" If you will descend to the ground floor," answered the old man, " my assistants will be happy to serve you with anything you may select. But the toys in this room I sell or keep as I please ! "

" What an obstinate old fool," thought the Stranger, " of course he says that thinking I'll pay some outrageous price," but aloud, he said : " Come, come, sir, you sold to my friend, Mr. Welcome, a doll similar to the one in that case. I do not understand your methods at all."

" Ah," said the old man, " Mr. Welcome understands my toys ; it is clear that you do not."

" What next shall I hear," growled the Stranger, with rising anger. " This is the most extraordinary place of business I've ever entered. You sell to this person and not to that. One client is received with open arms, another, such as myself, is insulted to his face. It's a crying scandal—an outrage on the public—I'll write to *The Times* about it—this very day . . ." He paused to take breath.

The old man became restless and spoke in a sad voice :

" You hinder me from my work. I must beg you to leave."

" How dare you ! " shouted the Stranger, his cheeks quivering from ill temper at not being able to obtain what he wanted for the first time in his life. " I've a very good mind to break my umbrella across your back, my man," and he began to shake the article in question in the old man's face. He uttered further threats of violence. As his anger increased, and his voice grew more and more strident and menacing, the old man became more and more agitated. His body shook, his arms and legs jerked spasmodically, he tried to speak but could not open his lips. He motioned wildly with his arms. Soon his head became affected with a peculiar tremor.

Seeing the old man weakening, as he thought, his tormentor redoubled his jibes.

" Is this necessary, all this shivering and shaking, because I've had to teach you your place ? " He gave a harsh laugh and sneered : " 'Pon my word, you look just like a stupid toy yourself."

At these words the old man trembled more convulsively than before ; his whole frame palpitated with extraordinary violence. Something creaked loudly, there was a discordant grinding noise, another creak, a whirr, and suddenly his head began slowly to turn right round on his neck. It continued to revolve with gathering speed. There was another grinding noise, followed by a sharp snap, when his head whizzed off his shoulders and crashed into the big glass case.

The Stranger, who had watched these extraordinary proceedings with mingled feelings of terror and amazement, gazed fearfully at the gaping neck from which protruded a bundle of metal filaments. " Good Heavens ! " he shouted, and, bolting from the room, he half-tumbled, half-slid, down the stairs. At the bottom he picked himself up, and, panting heavily, ran through the shop, which was empty save for the two assistants, who seemed to be attacked by some crisis of the nerves, for they were standing, shivering from head to foot, face to face behind the counter. The usual throng of customers had melted away, conscious that something was amiss and anxious, if their suspicions proved well founded, not to have their names cited in the papers in connection with it. The cause of all this trouble, bewailing the fact that he had come on foot, ran into Holborn, hailed a passing hansom and bade the cabby drive to his address as fast as he could go.

When the frightened customers had reached their separate homes, they found their children in tears, for none of their toys would work. And certain ladies and gentlemen who had purchased toys from the wonderful top floor found that these, too, would not work. One gentleman, a great lover of toys, was quite miserable when, on showing his collection to a friend, he found that not one would move.

" I can't understand it," he apologised, " I was always most careful not to strain the works."

" Well, well," said his wife, of a more practical turn of mind, " it's plain that nothing can be done to-night. To-morrow, you'd better take them to the shop and have them put right."

That next day—I wonder if it was ever forgotten by the inhabitants of that little street, and for how many years it provided a story to

be told after the Christmas dinner, when the bonbons had been pulled and the guests in their paper caps had battled with the fiery snapdragon ? At nine o'clock, the hour at which the shop usually opened, men, women and children of every station began to hasten from all points of the compass towards the familiar street. Some came in carriages, some in hansoms, but the majority came on foot.

Each person bore a parcel ; some heavy, some light ; some small, some large ; and the wrappings differed exceedingly, from clean brown paper to portions of an old and dirty apron. Soon the road was blocked from end to end, and the waiting rows of people began to extend into the side streets, far down Holborn and a considerable distance up Theobald's Road.

The shop was closed and the window shuttered, but the gay Christmas tree, with its tinkling bells, still swung above the doorway with each gust of wind. Those

nearest the shop pulled the bell and, receiving no answer, beat on the door with their bare fists. Minutes passed and the crowd steadily increased. The neighbours had their windows up, and, leaning out, shouted advice to those below.

" Perhaps they're ill," said some one.

" Better fetch a bobby," suggested another.

But already one was pushing his way down the street.

" What's all this about ? " he inquired.

On being told, he, too, pulled the bell and beat on the door. He went away and presently returned with a locksmith, who threw his bag on the ground and made a leisurely selection from his tools. The bystanders fidgeted with impatience while the workman prised the jamb with a cold chisel and probed the keyhole with bent pieces of wire.

Suddenly the door flew open ! There was a loud cheer and the crowd made a frenzied rush to see inside so that the policeman and

locksmith were thrown into the shop as if pro-
pelled from a cannon.

" Now then, steady there ! " gasped the
former.

But the crowd, unheeding, poured into the
shop and up the stairs to find—that each room
was completely empty.

.   .   .   .   .

" And what happened, then ? " asked Alice,
sitting at my feet.

" Ah ! *that*, my dear," I replied, " is another
story ! "

The End